HEADS IN THE SAND

By

Edna Lee Glines

©1990 by Edna Lee Glines

All rights reserved. No part of this book may be produced without the express written permission of the copyright holder. Permission is hereby granted to legitimate literary reviewers to reproduce excerpts in their reviews.

International Standard Book Number: 1–55666–041–3
Library of Congress Catalogue Card Number: 89–45464
Printed in the United States of America

Published in 1990 by
AUTHORS UNLIMITED
3324 Barham Blvd.
Los Angeles, CA 90068
(213) 874-0902

POLLY ON DUTY

TRANSFER OF PATIENTS

HIROSHIMA

Dedicated to the Memory of Polly, Dorothee,
Jane, and Ann, Navy Nurses of World War II

PREFACE

On June 12, 1988, a review of the documentary film, *Radio Bikini* by Ted Mahar, was published in the *Oregonian.* The members, and in particular Jeanne Gibson of the Eugene Writers' Group, brought it to my attention. They knew my sister had been at the Bikini Atoll when the bombs were exploded, and urged me to write about the explosions as they affected her life. This I have tried to do and am indebted to the following people:

Congressman Peter DeFazio for securing the war record of my sister, Lt. Commander Pauline Glines; The United States Navy and National Archives for material furnished; Ted Mahar, Portland *Oregonian* staff, for his review of the film documentary, *Radio Bikini* and his suggestion that I contact Robert Stone, Production, Ltd., Director of the film. Mr. Stone was very cooperative. Through him I was able to contact Dr. David Bradley, author of *No Place to Hide*, whose help and encouragement cannot be measured; Betta E. Harris for the many hours she has spent typing this script, and last but not least to Tom DeLigio for his beautiful poetry.

PROLOGUE

This is the true story of a beautiful young woman who answered the call of her country following Pearl Harbor. Aboard the hospital ship *Benevolence,* Polly was present when history was made. She was at Tokyo when the Japanese surrendered on September 2, 1945, and at the Bikini Atoll when the Atomic experiments were conducted, Abel Day, Monday, July 1, 1946 and on Baker Day, Thursday, July 25, 1946. The sunshine of her inner self overcame all adversity, including cancer, in a timeless love story. A few names have been changed to protect the innocent.

CONTENTS

BURIED ALIVE

Eloquent speeches,
leveled cities,
a hundred million cancers.
This nuclear wind
sings about all the windows,
reaches deep into the planet.

The politician, lobbying for more reactors
stands in a dark suit,
radiation crawling through his upper rooms—

The farmer in distant China
pausing in a rain-soaked field to pray,
his only child glowing underground.

This legacy of our greatest minds
slipping now, under every door,
circling everything we eat, touch
and love.

For as long as there are borders, walls
and plutonium,
for as long as we breathe in hatred,
for as long as we fear
and fail to see beauty,
that true and dazzling light
in every soul.

Tom DeLigio

CHAPTER 1

The United Airlines Stewardess

Twenty year old Pauline Glines (Polly), registered nurse and stewardess for United Airlines, sat at the dressing room table in the bathroom alcove of her apartment. She was enjoying the solitude and quiet of the apartment located on the shores of Lake Michigan. She yawned and stretched as she relaxed, critically examining her image in the mirror. A beautiful young woman was this–full red lips and dark brown hair framing a near perfect face. At the center of that face, like a magnet, were two soft brown eyes reflecting love for all the world and its inhabitants, man, plant and animal. She loved life and it seemed to love her. As she examined her profile, her thoughts returned to her just completed interview.

He must have liked me, she thought. "He" being Rick Masters, Director of Personnel, United Airlines. After deliberating for an hour, or so it seemed to Polly, he had said, "You're hired. However, we may have to put lifts on your shoes since you are one-half inch below job specifications. I am stretching a point in hiring you. Perhaps we can discuss this over dinner tonight?"

"Yes," replied Polly. She was thrilled to become a stewardess—a much sought after position by nurses in 1940. The main requirement for a stewardess was that she be a registered nurse, since nausea and other illnesses were very common in the unpressurized cabins of the tough riding, small planes. A nurse was kept busy on most flights. Polly

1

was so happy to have a job that she bubbled over and smiled at one and all as she rode the El toward her apartment. Getting off at her stop, she walked a few steps, then danced a few as she twirled toward her apartment.

Now, as she sat in her dressing room, reliving the interview with Rick Masters, she happily hummed to music coming from her radio. All was right in her world. Then suddenly music and humming stopped. A feeling of apprehension filled the room.

"We interrupt this program to bring you the following speech delivered by Adolph Hitler to his troops in Austria—"

Polly, startled, listened. In the years ahead, she would never forget the shrill voice of the madman, Hitler, nor the response to that voice. In unison thousands of voices shouted, "HEIL HITLER! HEIL HITLER! HEIL HITLER!" This was followed by the deafening roar of stomping boots. Over and over came the shrill exhortation from Hitler, followed by the same tumultuous response. Terrifying!

Cold chills permeated Polly's entire being. They're crazy! They're all crazy, she thought—then she, as did other Americans, buried her head in the sand.

Back to her bath she went. "Into the tub I must go-go-go," sang the lovely young maiden, as she drew her bath adding lots of bubble bath. "Heaven is lined with bubbles I know-know-know." Then slowly, softly she sank into the luxurious suds.

When bottom was reached, she alternately stretched each leg toward heaven, sensually stroking them as she did so. "Not bad, not bad at all," she said to herself, purring like a kitten.

She was brought from her heaven to earth by the sound of voices. Her three roommates had returned from their shopping spree, where no doubt they had spent their month's salary. The three of them, Jane Moe, Ann Scott, and Kate Rose came from small towns and, as usually is the case, Chicago with its choice of clothes overwhelmed them. Jane, Polly's favorite, came into the dressing room, a new dress on each arm.

"Watch out, Jane, don't get too close. I might ruin your new dresses," said a very wet Polly, blowing bubbles from her nose.

2

Drawing the dress from danger, Jane asked, "Would you like to wear one of these tonight? You have a date, don't you?"

"Yes, Mr. Masters from United gave me a job and asked me out to dinner. He said we needed to discuss my responsibilities. However, it won't be necessary to borrow your new dress. I bought one in Oklahoma City when I was there. I think Rick will like it."

And indeed Rick did like it and the package within. "How beautiful you are!" he exclaimed when she emerged for their date. "Let me look at you." Her pink, raw silk dress enhanced the flush on her olive skin and was just short enough to reveal the well-sculptured, self-admired legs of her bubble bath. Rick turned her around in open admiration. Polly did not mind—she liked this man!

Leaving the others, Rick escorted her to his 1939 Oldsmobile. The new car smell was still present.

"My, this is a nice car," said Polly. "I bought an old clunker as soon as I had enough money after graduating from nurse's training. I sold it just before I came to Chicago. This is nice." She sighed with contentment as she rubbed the velvety texture of the upholstery.

"I had one like that, too, before I bought this," said Rick. "I'm glad that I have it for you." As the car purred on, Rick said, "Polly, tell me about yourself. You seem so very different from most of the women I know. I am entranced."

"Well," said Polly, "are you sure you want to hear this? My father and mother were country school teachers and I lived most of my life in the country. We didn't have much money, but there was lots of love. We were all willing to sacrifice for one another. I'm like my mother, or so they tell me. I am the baby of the family of ten—four in my immediate family, two half-sisters and two half-brothers. I, of course, don't think I am spoiled. We learned to take care of ourselves very early in life. Mother was just too busy teaching and keeping house. We walked over two miles to and from school in all kinds of weather. My sister, four years older than I, was a second mother to me, often escorting me home from school. She and a half-sister paid my expenses through nursing school, and here I am. Now tell me about you."

Rick sighed. "Now I know why you are so different and lovely. I wish my family had been large like yours. I am an

3

only child. My father died eight years ago. Mother has remarried a very fine man. They live in Florida–Jacksonville. I graduated from the University of Florida, learned to fly, and was a pilot until two years ago. Flying was bothering my ears. I was afraid of deafness, so I took this job which I like very much."

Rick maneuvered the Oldsmobile in front of the Blackstone Hotel, where a parking attendant took over. Inside were candle lit tables and soft dance music. The tune "You Are The One" pervaded the room and the couple's senses. They danced on and on, never really discussing Polly's stewardess duties.

In the months ahead, Polly learned her duties as the spokes of United Airline's giant wheel spun round and round, sending her and other young nurses to every major city in the United States. In between the cities lay vast expanses of land, partially inhabited, but mostly uninhabited and always varied. Looking at the checkerboard farms from the air was entrancing, especially the red, red soil of Oklahoma alternating with the green pastures. Polly eagerly looked down. This had been her childhood home.

A major delight to Polly was to see the shapes of the fast-moving shadows cast on the ground by sun and clouds. She let her imagination run amok. What sort of monster was that? Is that an Indian brave riding his horse? Is that not a herd of buffalo?

The young women, being full of life, were delighted with the Pacific Ocean, its coastline and its cities, especially that jewel of the west, San Francisco. The Golden Gate swung open, giving its heart to the nurses–an act which was to be repeated over and over in the next five years.

CHAPTER II

Pearl Harbor

Through the ages, power hungry men have led other men by oratory as though they were sheep, led them to the abyss and into war. Such men were Adolph Hitler and Benito Mussolini. Working together, they ran over country after country, toppling France's famous Magino Line like toothpicks.

From across the English Channel came a powerful voice to counteract them, one of the world's most famous orators, Winston Churchill. In the voice which captured the hearts of all Britons, he declared, "You ask, what is our policy? I will say: It is to wage war, by sea, land, and air, with all our might and with all the strength that God can give us; to wage war against a monstrous tyranny, never surpassed in the dark, lamentable catalogue of human crime. That is our policy. You ask, what is our aim? I can answer in one word: Victory–victory at all costs, victory in spite of all terror, victory, however long and hard the road may be; for without victory, there is no survival." His countrymen arose to fight until death or victory.

In 1940, another voice arose, that of Franklin Roosevelt, the powerful president of the United States. He was so angry on hearing that Mussolini had attacked France that he declared for all the world to hear, "The hand that holds the dagger has stabbed his neighbor in the back!" From then on, it was only a matter of time until the U.S.A. would come to the aid of England and France.

5

Following the debacle of Dunkirk, many Americans were sure that the U.S. would soon enter the war. One of these was Rick Masters. He called Polly and asked her to meet him in New York City. There, after wining and dining–a lot of wining on Rick's part–he gained the courage to say, "I am sure we will be in the war before long, and since I am a registered pilot, I will be one of the first to be conscripted. I am going to register before I am called." He reached across the table, taking Polly's hand. "You must know how very much I love you, my darling. Will you marry me before I have to go?"

Polly was not ready to answer. With her unimprisoned hand she gently patted his cheek and said, "Perhaps some day, Rick, but I'm not ready for marriage now. If we do get into war with those Germans, I will be needed as a nurse." She shuddered as she remembered the shrill voice of Hitler and the answering thunder of his storm troopers.

That evening before they separated, Rick held Polly close, so close that breathing for her was difficult. Desire for her made Rick shake, so much so his voice trembled. "Are you sure?"

"I don't know what I want right now, Rick," replied Polly, "but if and when I marry you, I want everything to be normal."

"You are right, I know, but I will try again and again," said Rick.

Then the thunderbolt struck. The walls of isolation came thundering down. In a sneak attack, the Japanese hit Pearl Harbor, sending ships and men to a watery grave. A major part of the mighty U.S. Navy was gone or crippled.

Bewilderment and anger prevailed across the country as the mighty giant that is the United States of America, raised its head from the sand. Overnight, from Seattle to San Diego, blackout curtains covered windows. Dark was the country, but not the spirit of her people. Instead, in the breast of every American citizen was the resolve to atone for this insult to his or her country.

Frenzied was the action and reaction in the following weeks as men and women rushed to enlist. Rick was among the first, and was asked to report immediately to Edwards Air Force Base. Holding Polly close before leaving, he said with tears in his eyes, "It is hell to leave you, but I know you are right. It would be worse if we were married."

Polly's arms tightened around his neck and tears streamed down her face. Had she made the right decision?

Polly, Jane, Ann, and Kate had just finished a communal dinner, washed and wiped the dishes and now were having a communal discussion. The topic was enlisting for the wartime service.

Jane said, "A physical education teacher friend of mine signed up with the intention of being a physical therapist. They put her in charge of a beer commissary in Florida. Nurses are needed very much, so I don't think they will do that to us."

Kate knew what her answer had to be. She said, "I can't leave my mother. She isn't at all well and Dad isn't able to take care of her. I will have to stay in the States where I can be reached at all times. I will just be a civilian nurse. We will need plenty of those."

Polly said, "I read an article saying how much the women nurses have meant to the wounded in Europe. It seems they are a 'mother figure', and although we are not old enough to be their mothers, I guess nurses are angels of mercy to them and they turn to us as they would turn to their mothers. I am going home for awhile to think it over. Jane, why don't you come home with me?"

"I will," replied Jane. "If we decide to enlist let's do it together. Polly, did you read about the hospital ship, *Solace*, that was at Pearl Harbor when the Japanese crippled our navy? Here it is. Let me read it to you:

'The hospital ship, *Solace*, was resting at Pearl Harbor the morning of December 7, 1941, when Japanese planes swooped down and started bombing and strafing. The head nurse on the *Solace* was Lieutenant Commander Grace B. Lally, a veteran nurse.

'Miss Lally looked out a porthole and saw young men being machine gunned as they tried to escape. She knew what was happening, as this veteran of twenty-two years in the Naval Nurse Corps, had seen this in the China war with Japan. She immediately set up an emergency ward to treat

7

those being fished out of the water, covered with oil, many extensively burned. Some were brought in from nearby ships severely wounded.

'There were twelve nurses aboard the *Solace*, most of whom had never experienced war-time duty. Some might have collapsed under the strain, had it not been for the courage and example set for them by Commander Lally. As bombs hit the *Arizona*, anchored next to them, the nurses treated 327 burn cases that first day.

'The *Solace* was constantly in danger, being so close to the *Battleship Arizona*. Somehow the navy managed to move the *Solace* before the *Arizona* exploded and went down. She remained in Pearl Harbor, her medical corps treating the burned and wounded for ten days.

'The wounded men gathered courage and solace from the nurses and seemed more interested in the welfare of their comrades than in themselves. "Help him first" and "God bless you, ma'am," were heard over and over.' "

CHAPTER III

Basic Training

Like explorers of old, Polly and Jane left the old life to face the dangers of the new. They now were on their way to San Diego for basic training. Ann had been sent to the East Coast. Polly sat at the window of their train, looking out, but not seeing the scenery which had enamored her in the previous weeks. She was very quiet.

"What's the matter, Polly?" asked Jane. "You are so quiet."

"Jane, I'm scared. Can I take this? I can't even swim!" replied Polly.

Jane said, "You are one of the bravest people I know, and as for swimming, the ocean is so big, none of us could swim to safety unless we were very close to shore. Come on, Polly, let's face it, you would have hundreds of sailors jumping overboard to save you."

Polly grinned as she hugged her friend. "Oh, Jane, I don't know what I would do without you. When I think of what we are facing, I want to run!"

"We all do," said Jane.

Then Polly reverted to a practice of her childhood. She pulled down a mental curtain to block out unpleasant thoughts. Playfully, she said, "I painted my fingernails red this morning. Thought it might be the last time for awhile. Our drill sergeant will probably object to red fingernails. I put on extra cologne, too. Do you think I should walk slowly

9

past that good looking officer sitting by the aisle? He is studying that manual so diligently. He needs a break!"

Jane snorted. "Polly, Rick isn't here to protect you and I think you just may get into trouble, if you don't watch out."

Polly again became quiet. How would it be to see broken bodies, some with parts missing on young men in the promise of youth? Could she draw a mental curtain on her own pain and give them the love, encouragement, and medical care necessary? "God, please help me," she silently prayed.

It was at least fifteen minutes before the mood returned to walk past the officer. He looked up, then looked again and again. Gone was his concentration.

The DC3 carrying the two nurses circled out over the ocean before approaching Lindbergh Field. From overhead came the droning sounds of many planes protecting the harbor and naval base. It would be a long time before the lesson of Pearl Harbor would be forgotten. On landing, the girls discovered that fellow passengers were mostly other nurses with the same destination.

When the Chief Nurse met them, they felt right at home. All during their hospital training they had been supervised by a Chief Nurse. She looked at Polly and said, "So you are Miss Glines." Polly wondered why, but one does not question a Chief Nurse. When she arrived in her quarters on the naval base she understood why. Greeting her was a large bouquet of roses with a note reading, "Cannot get leave now. I am on duty twenty-four hours a day. Will plan on flying there some weekend before long. Much love, Rick."

A warm glow filled Polly's heart. How wonderful was this man! Since she had met him, he had done everything possible to make life easier for her. Am I in love? she asked herself. They say I will know, so I guess I'm not.

The next morning Polly awakened to a day enveloped with a cold fog. She snuggled down, drawing the not so pretty, but very warm navy blanket around her. According to the natives and the Chief Nurse, the San Diego weather was the best in the United States. Polly discovered this to be true. The fog burned off before 10:00 a.m. that morning and glittering diamonds shimmered on the waters of the bay.

Polly's basic training was vigorous, although not nearly as vigorous as that of the army nurse, whose life sometimes depended upon her physical stamina. The navy nurse was required to drill, perform calisthenics and even climb over and down the high net (which was part of the obstacle course). The army nurse was required to hike six miles in two hours. Later she also hiked twelve miles in seven hours carrying a gas mask, knapsack and a canteen full of water, stopping after the first six miles for a gas mask drill.

The navy nurse learned to climb the obstacle net so that should the occasion arise, she could climb from the ocean to the deck of her ship.

Both the navy nurse and army nurse had classes in military courtesy, protection against chemical warfare, along with the latest techniques in preventing and treating disease.

A definite schedule was planned with definite ideas concerning what to do and when to do it. It was self explanatory, and having a routine to follow immediately made each nurse feel as though she belonged.

Navy terminology was in constant use, and after the first morning, "Hit the deck" sounded as natural as "Get up." All were glad to have the opportunity to take an orientation course before going on duty. There are always a thousand and one questions concerning navy nursing, and they are all answered in various lectures and movies given in an indoctrination course. Thus, when the nurse goes on duty, she feels well equipped to do efficient nursing the navy way.

Drill every day from 13:00–15:00 (1–3 p.m.) was something new and different. It took timing, cooperation, practice and a clear knowledge of right from left hand. All were quite surprised by the end result. During the three weeks she is a 'boot', the nurse attends classes in Naval Customs and Traditions, navy Rules and Regulations, Ward Management and Naval Hospital Procedures. The nurse is given survival training. She has a tour of sickbay aboard a ship (a thrilling experience for the nurse). Finally outfitted in complete uniform, she stands for inspection by her Commanding Officer. She has become a navy Nurse, ready for duty.

During their three weeks of basic training, many letters were received by the two nurses. Excerpts and a letter follow:

To Polly from her sister in Oregon:

"Will work this week and next with other teachers issuing ration stamps. This will be done after school hours.

The urge to create life instead of destroying it is abounding in our high school. I fear many pregnancies. Had one girl come to me crying–afraid she was pregnant. I sent her to her own doctor. False alarm! Next time?

Am glad I have good tires on my car as I hear they must last for the duration. I live 4½ miles from school and there is no public transportation here. May have to ride the school bus. A lot of the women teachers are driving them."

To Jane from her father in Missouri:

"Am glad you are a good swimmer, since you joined the navy.

Feel sorry for your brother. He was classified 4F and feels inferior."

To Jane from her mother in Missouri:

"Your father misses you so very much and is concerned for your welfare.

He also misses baseball games. They have been curtailed.

It was so hot here yesterday, we experienced a phenomenon. I heard a pop-pop-pop in the kitchen. Went there and discovered three glasses had broken from the heat. I never heard of such a thing!"

1400 Westwood Ave.
Los Angeles, Ca.
June 15, 1942

"Dear Polly:

It is possible I will see you before long. With the gasoline stamps I had hoarded for months, I managed to drive down to L.A. for summer school. Yes, even in war time, there is a requirement that we attend summer school. I hope I manage to get enough stamps from the ration board here to return home. The government should give me extra stamps as I brought two high school graduates down with me to work in aircraft factories. There is a demand for women welders. It seems their smaller hands can reach into small areas men cannot reach.

"I must tell you about driving down here in 'blackout' conditions. We were all right the first day, as we reached our destination during daylight hours. But on the second day, we were at least two hours out of L.A., when it became dark. We could not use lights, of course, but did manage to drive safely. We got behind a big transport truck and let him guide us in. He must have really known that highway. All he used were his parking lights, which were directed downward.

"When we arrived here I was surprised by many things. The service stations are nearly all of them operated by women–very few men. There are a few stations where an older man is supervising, mostly where there is a garage or repair shop attached.

"One misses the sound of little children playing. The children cannot lead normal lives since mother or father may be sleeping during the daytime–sometimes both, having worked a 'graveyard' shift. Grandmother, or sometimes grandfather, is baby sitting the children. Even with their help, workers are often awakened by excess noise or excess light. Many use 'blinders' and ear plugs in order to sleep.

"In the small town in Oregon where I teach, we do not have these things with which to cope. However, we do have our share of grief. It has been necessary to cope with the death of several young men. Just before I drove down, we received notice of the death of one of the members of the football team. I spent hours trying to console his girlfriend.

13

She feels close to me and came to me for help. I hope I did.

"One thing we have had in Oregon, that I believe has occurred nowhere else–the Japanese dropped fire bombs on the coastal forests. They might have succeeded in causing major fire damage, however, they did not know about weather in Oregon. There had been abnormally hot weather in the interior of the state, and when that is true, dense fog is on the coast. The fog was deep enough that day to soak the fire bombs and douse the fire.

"Now, my darling sister, I must end this letter (long for me) with a 'funny'–('tis funny to me, but not to Silver). You remember Silver, my Chow dog. I brought her down here with me, and take her for a walk every morning. She is so good and comes right along with me–needs no leash. Sometimes she comes so close to me she almost pushes me over. That is because the mocking birds dive bomb her if she strays from my side. They gang up on her, aiming primarily for that plume of tail.

"Will try to get another letter to you before you are 'out there' where I cannot communicate with you very well. Much love, and God be with you!

Your sister,

Edna"

It was drill time–not a happy time for Jane. "I am a klutz," she said. She does lack physical coordination, thought Polly, but it does not affect her brain. I would not trade her for anyone, except perhaps one of my sisters. Today they hoped Jane would perform better. If not, it would not be for lack of effort. Polly had given the commands and they had drilled and drilled Jane in their room. So realistic were the commands–"right face, left face, forward march and to the rear march"–that the Chief Nurse had come to see what was going on. She laughed, gave them encouragement and left. On this particular day Jane did very well, very well indeed. They were so charged up after their success that on their way

14

back to quarters, Polly ran to the obstacle course where that high box covered with net stood. Up, up she climbed, but suddenly stopped. The box talked. "Oh, damn!" Polly had broken a fingernail. Only for a moment, however, did she stop her assault.

Jane yelled, "Polly, get down. Don't do that when you don't have to!"

"Okay! Okay! I'm coming. There comes the sergeant, anyway. Let's do a quick disappearing act."

When they reached their quarters Polly was a full twenty yards ahead of Jane. They hurried to their room, knowing the sergeant would not come in after them. They couldn't lose their leave! They were having dinner tonight at the Officer's Club with Rick and a fellow officer of his.

Their cab had arrived early, so the young nurses sat in the lobby of the large waiting room. Both giggled when Polly asked, "Shall we practice your marching? It's larger here than in our room." Then both girls gasped. Across the large room came Rick with his friend—the good looking officer with whom Polly had flirted!

"Oh, my!" muttered Jane. "I hope he doesn't recognize you!"

When Rick introduced them to Dave Merrill, the man did not act as though he had met them—and indeed he had not—but Polly was sure he recognized the flirtatious nurse whom he had seen on the airplane. Thank God he is a gentleman, she thought.

Near the entrance to the dining room stood a "one-armed bandit" (slot machine). First Rick, then Dave put in a quarter. They repeated their act until each had been robbed of two dollars, then stopped. Polly said, "Now you two just watch." She winked at Rick and put in a quarter—no deal. She put in another quarter. Clang, clang went the machine as it rolled up three cherries, and out came ten dollars!

"Hey, give me back my money!" cried Rick.

"No way!" answered Polly, as she and Jane scooped the quarters into their purses.

CHAPTER IV

On Leave

Basic training was over for those nurses who had enlisted soon after Pearl Harbor. A short leave was theirs now, before reporting to Cedar Rapids, Iowa for Naval Hospital Training.

In the early morning they awaited the Atchison, Topeka, and Santa Fe train which at that time ran from San Diego through Dallas, Oklahoma City and on to St. Louis. The long mournful wail cried to hundreds of couples engaged in long, long farewell embraces as they lined up alongside the tracks. The conductor shook his head as he called, "All aboard." He would never get used to the line of sailors who always managed to have a girl in the port of San Diego.

Down the line of couples Jane spotted the good looking Dave Merrill who appeared to be in charge of a group of hospital corpsmen. Admiring him, Jane said "He told me that he is a doctor. Did Rick tell you that?"

"No, but I'm sure we will find out on this long trip. I think we will find out about a lot of things," said Polly.

Around noon the train reached the great American desert. A wasteland of sand was all that could be seen in every direction. Heat waves shimmered upward and in the distance was the ever present mirage looking like water in some form—a running stream or a lake. Sometimes an oasis appeared surrounded by trees. It was easy to understand how people, stranded in the desert, went mad when time and time again the mirage proved to be a hoax.

17

Polly turned to Jane. "I haven't seen a car on that highway over there for over thirty minutes. No wonder the natives always carry a five gallon can of water in the car. My sister had a heat stroke on this desert a few years ago. She was driving from San Diego to Oklahoma City. I wonder if it was along here. It seems a likely place. I'm sure grateful for this air conditioned train. We are lucky to be on one."

"Yes, we are lucky," replied Jane.

The journey of three days and three nights to Oklahoma City was long and tiresome, but not nearly so much for the nurses as for the corpsmen. The nurses had a seat at all times, whereas the corpsmen did not. While some corpsmen sat, others walked the aisles or sat on the floor. Most were boys from Texas, and did not seem to resent that the women had the best of everything. Southern chivalry prevailed.

The seats became sleeping berths at night, a lower and an upper. Jane and Polly shared an upper birth where they dressed and undressed. It would have been difficult to go to the bathroom at night, but fortunately they did not need to. When they undressed, the porter asked from outside the curtains, "Press your uniforms, ladies?" They were only too happy to pay for this service as it meant four less objects in their tight sleeping quarters.

During the last day a porter brought a newspaper to them. The whole front page read of the Bataan Death March in which 750,000 prisoners of war, many severely wounded, had to walk for six days, 140 miles, without food or water. If a man fell and another tried to help him, the second man was beaten so much he could scarcely stand up.

"Jane, do you think Americans would do this?" Polly was aghast as she read The San Diego Union's description of one of history's most nauseating records of man's inhumanity to man—the Bataan Death March.

"I'm not sure, Polly. War causes us to forget all the 'civilized' values we have learned, and revert to our savage ancestors. The idea seems to be to make the enemy suffer as much as possible—even little children. Of course horror tales are told by each side to increase war intensity. I can remember that during World War I the 'huns' were accused of cutting off little children's heads. That was not true, but I am afraid some of the tales of the extermination of Jews at the present time may be true."

"I wonder," said Polly, "why the Japanese seem to hate us so much? What have we done to them?"

Jane then said, "I have no idea why they hate us so much. I have never had anything against the Japanese people, but I do after this death march!"

"I cry for Maria and the other nurses who were captured at Corregidor. Maria was in nurse's training with me. Did I tell you that?" said Polly.

"No, I didn't know," answered Jane.

"I am afraid she and others will suffer the worst indignities, including rape, that a man can impose on a woman. Oh, Maria!" sobbed Polly.

"When did you last hear from her?" asked Jane.

"Just before the fall of Corregidor. Somehow she got a letter out just prior to that, probably through a native. Most of the letter was spent telling me about her cat 'Cory' named for Corregidor. During the siege for that fortress, when the Japanese began shelling, Maria would put a helmet on herself and would put Cory in a helmet. As the shelling continued, Cory did not wait for Maria—he ran to his own helmet and crawled in for protection. Poor Cory, I wonder what will happen to him now?"

Jane felt like laughing and crying. "There are a few things at which we can laugh, even in war. A cat that intelligent will somehow manage to survive, I believe—provided the Japanese do not eat him."

The train now approached Texas and, although both nurses had grown up in the south, they were disturbed when they heard one of the Texas corpsmen say, "I told that porter that we would get him when we crossed the Texas line." There was really no need for Jane and Polly to worry about the porter. He knew how to take care of himself. He had completely disappeared when the train reached the Texas border.

As the train moved on to Oklahoma City, Polly recognized familiar sights. When they reached her home town, she stepped off into the arms of the few family members still living there. Jane continued on to St. Louis, her home. Each day of leave would be savored before moving on in their wartime service.

CHAPTER V

Cedar Falls and Bethesda Naval Hospitals

The fragile coral of youth
shattered, like panes of glass
beneath a storm of bombs.
Only courage, that lion within,
walks beside us here.

After a year's training at Cedar Falls Naval Hospital in Iowa, Polly's probation period, as a reserve nurse ended and she was appointed Nurse, U.S.N. Orders were received to report to Bethesda Naval Hospital, Baltimore, Maryland for further training.

From the European Theater of Combat came the knowledge that thousands of lives could be saved if the war casualties received medical attention immediately after being wounded. The U.S. Medical Service acted on this knowledge. Medical corpsmen followed the G.I. closely into battle; hospital ships were not far behind the ships of war; and occasionally a fleet plane, with medical help aboard, would come to the aid of the severely wounded. The miracle drugs, sulpha and penicillin, were now in use, preventing the amputations of World War I. At Bethesda Naval Hospital, Maryland, nurses and corpsmen gained access to the best in surgical methods.

All was not work, however. New friends were made and many social events scheduled. One new friend for Polly and

Jane was Alice Holt from Boston. She was a delight to know, such fun, and always kept them laughing. She had another big asset–seemingly she knew all the men on base and willingly introduced them to her new friends. Polly and Jane could choose a new date each night if they so wished–and they generally did. This new duty proved to be very pleasant.

Then a dark cloud closed in on Polly and Jane's world. One summer night lightning flashed and thunder reverberated throughout the huge hospital. Polly, who was on duty, shivered. She never had liked thunder storms. To bolster her courage, she left the nurse's station to look in on her patients. They encouraged her as much or more than she did them, especially one young man who had lost a leg. He was very philosophical about it and looked forward to being fitted with an artificial one. He laughingly talked her out of her anxiety. Feeling better, having checked her patients, Polly decided to walk down the long corridor to the station where, undisturbed by the storm, Alice sat checking her records.

Polly interrupted her. "Hi, Alice, how can you sit there like that in this terrible storm?"

Alice did not laugh as usual. "I was finishing these records before I left," she answered. "Now I must check on my patients. Good-bye, Polly. I mean good-night."

The thunder cracked again, and Polly reacted as though she had been hit. And indeed she had been hit–she received one of life's major blows that night. Alice committed suicide.

The next morning Polly was called into the Head Surgeon's office. What had she done? Many navy officials were present, including the Chief Nurse who said, "Miss Glines, we have some very bad news for you. Miss Holt died last night from an apparent heart attack." Polly gasped, then regained her composure. "We have chosen you, since we believe you to be very discreet, to accompany the body to Boston. We will make all the arrangements. You are to be in dress uniform at all times so I have ordered three additional white dress uniforms for you. We know this is a sad and demanding experience, but it may be rewarding to you to know that we think you can handle this responsibility better than any other nurse. We talked to Miss Holt's parents this morning and they wished for you to come. They said Miss Holt had mentioned you as a 'special friend'."

The train ride seemed endless as Polly accompanied Alice's body to Boston. She visited the bathroom several times to shed tears. She longed for one of her own family to be with her. How I wish there were someone here in whom I could confide, she said to herself. I am sure Alice did not have a heart attack. She hinted to me that she might be pregnant and knowing that her physical was coming soon, I'm sure she feared a dishonorable discharge. The only person I could tell would be my sister if she were here. I can't even tell Jane.

When Polly arrived in Boston, Mrs. Holt sobbingly asked, "How did it happen, Polly? Were you there?"

All Polly could do was to shake her head, no. She could not speak.

"I'm glad you were the one to bring her home. She thought a lot of you," said the grieving mother.

In spite of the grief wrenching her own heart, Polly was glad, too.

On the return trip from Boston to Baltimore, Polly had much time for thought. Oh, Alice, why did you do it? We could have found some way out other than this. I don't know just what–but something!

In her deep thoughts Polly was oblivious to her surroundings until disturbed by a familiar voice.

"May I sit here?"

"Yes" replied Polly, then looked up into the familiar face of Eleanor Roosevelt, who quietly took Polly's hand, told her how beautiful she looked in her white uniform and how proud she was of her–then left.

Polly never knew why Mrs. Roosevelt was on the train, if she was aware of Polly's mission, if it was her purpose to ease the turmoil in the young nurse's heart–or if she was just being Eleanor Roosevelt.

Polly was ever so happy to have two letters from her sister waiting for her upon her return to Bethesda Hospital:

"Dear Polly:

I know you will not be able to receive very many letters when you are at sea, nor will I be able to talk freely, so am writing more while you are in the U.S. I never have written so many letters in such a short time. The incidents may be boring, compared with the things happening to you, but I think you will enjoy the following:

"*Incident #1:* It was 11:30 p.m. last Friday night and we, Betta and I, were fast asleep, or at least I was, when Betta whispered in my ear, 'Wake up! Wake up! Someone is in the front room.'

"I sleepily said, 'Oh, you are imagining things. Go back to sleep.' However, something told me to listen. I heard something rubbing against the front room wall. Now, Polly, you remember the old hockey stick O.C.W. presented me when I graduated? Well, I always keep it handy by my bed, just in case. Can you imagine anything worse than being hit over the head with one of those sticks? So, now being sure I might need it, I whispered to Betta, 'You slip out the side door over there and call the police. If anyone comes in here, I will hit him over the head with my hockey stick.'

"Just then a voice came from the front room. 'Betta, are you awake? This is Nora. Sure am glad you left the front room door unlocked. I thought I could sleep here on the davenport. Sorry, didn't mean to wake you up. I would have been here hours ago, but was bumped in Roseburg by two soldiers on their way to Ft. Lewis.'

"Holding up the hockey stick, I said, 'Nora, you scared us silly. It is a good thing you didn't come in here. You probably would have been hit over the head with this.'

" 'Oh, my!' responded Nora, rubbing her head. 'That would have been the end of me. I'll knock on the door next time.'

24

"Incident #2: Nora lived far from any indication that a war was raging. She had her own cow for butter and milk, her own beef and chickens to eat, a garden full of fresh vegetables and a pantry full of canned fruits and vegetables. She received more gasoline ration stamps than most, since her home was thirty some miles from Grants Pass. Her home was indeed a paradise, located on the Illinois River, a tributary of the famous Rogue River. The reason for telling this is to give her an alibi for buying a pound of butter the next day thus using most of our ration stamps which we had been hoarding for special occasions. Buying that butter made us go meatless for the rest of the month. Oh, well, it didn't hurt us. It just meant that having real butter we would not have to stir coloring into margarine so that it would look like butter instead of lard.

All our love,

Edna"

367 W. 13th Ave.
Eugene, Or.
April 15, 1945

"Dear Polly:

You will be leaving soon. I want to get this to you before you go. I must tell you about our trip to the coast last week. We have been unable to go there for a year due to the rationing of gasoline. The four of us who have cars, saved our stamps by walking every place we went for over a month.

"The only car safe enough to drive that far (because of tires) belongs to me—a Dodge coupe. How could we take seven people plus baggage? Well, we borrowed a luggage carrier for the roof of the car, cut boards to brace the trunk top open so that it would not fall on us, and loaded up—four of us in the trunk: Our sister Helen, Ione, Gloria and I. Three sat in the front seat: Betta (the driver), Nora and Jessie. We took as little baggage as possible, so that it would go in the cartop carrier.

"We drove north of Eugene and turned west through Corvallis so that those who had never seen the Oregon Coast could see as much as our ration stamps would allow. When we arrived at Newport we expected to see many 'vacancy' signs, but most of the signs read, 'Closed for the duration'. Finally, one of us spied a motel, somewhat off the highway, with lights on and a small sign reading 'Vacancy'. We drove as fast as possible down a sharp incline to the motel. When we rang the door-bell and no one answered for several minutes, our hearts stood still. Then the door opened with a bang and in the doorway stood a young man, almost naked. Around his waist was a towel. Perhaps he had come from his shower. We never knew.

"He said, 'The only unit left is next door, but it has only two double beds.'

" 'We'll take it,' we all said in unison. The blankets we had used to cushion our seats in the car trunk would now serve as mattresses on the floor. The beds had excess covers which could be borrowed by the 'floor sleepers'. We drew straws to see which four would sleep on the beds, and I lucked out. Poor Nora and two others slept on the floor!

"Before going to bed, we ate the excellent stew Nora had made. Somehow she had wheedled our butcher out of enough beef for seven people. Betta had made two apple pies, so with the addition of two loaves of garlic bread (with Nora's ration stamp butter), no one went hungry.

"We were getting ready for bed, when the 'naked' young man from next door came over, now completely dressed. He asked, 'Would one of you young ladies like to accompany me to the town dance tonight?' We were all tired from our trip, and also wary of 'towel draper', so all said no.

"When he had gone, Nora said, 'The craziest things go on in Eugene. Yesterday I saw a long line of people down town and joined them to see what they were getting. I hoped it might be a pound of butter, but then, after being in line for nearly an hour, all I was able to buy was a package of cigarettes. I decided to charge 50¢ for the package even though it cost me only 25¢. I guess my time is worth 25¢ an hour. I asked Helen if she wanted them. Now, cigarettes are difficult to buy and Helen was glad to pay 50¢.

"Next morning while packing, the young man appeared to see if we were staying another night. Nora whispered, 'Do you suppose that if I stood in every Eugene line, he might be a prize in one of them? How much would Helen pay for him?'

"Trips to the coast being rare, we decided to see as much as possible. We drove south to Cape Perpetua. Helen and Ione had never seen the Oregon Coast and were in awe of the long span of rugged coast line seen from the apex of Cape Perpetua. We were all thrilled by the appearance of a dirigible patrolling the coast looking for the possible appearance of an enemy submarine. It was such a beautiful day. The sky was so blue and peaceful looking, one could not realize that to the west a war was raging and men were being killed. We waved at the dirigible and the pilot dipped the nose of the giant ship. As we looked down we saw one of the coast's most spectacular sights–The Devil's Elbow–where the waves are churned into a coast alcove with such force, a massive geyser is shot into the air.

"As we walked down the mountain, leaving the scene, I noticed Helen and Ione smoking Nora's ration line cigarettes. Coming from the Midwest they did not realize the damage just one of those dropped in the dry grass of a forest can do. An ignorant smoker can accomplish what the Japanese had been unable to do with their fire baloons–that is, set fire to the forests of the Oregon Coast. I followed them so that I could step on any spark they might drop. No harm was done.

"From Cape Perpetua we drove on down to the Sea Lion Caves where hundreds of the massive animals come in for shelter. The sight of so many in their natural habitat is unforgettable, but believe me their smell is also unforgettable!

"I thought of you so many times, wishing you could be with us. Somehow, I would have squeezed you into the trunk—or left someone at home.

Much, much love,

Edna"

CHAPTER VI

The *U.S.S. Benevolence*

On May 12, 1945 the time arrived for Polly and Jane to join hospital ships for the duration of the war. The girls shivered and drew their warm navy capes around them to shut out the chill of the morning fog of San Francisco Bay. They were quiet, very quiet as the moment of separation neared. A fog horn issued a mournful call to add to the gloom. Among the hundreds of gray ship forms in the distance were their ships: Polly's the *U.S.S. Benevolence* and Jane's the *U.S.S. Bountiful.* Little did Polly realize that soon she would fall in love with her ship. However, Jane would receive a different assignment when she reached Pearl Harbor.

"When our transportation comes, let's separate quickly, then we will not have to think about it," said Jane.

"Okay," said Polly, wanting to cry, but not doing so.

Soon ship to shore boats arrived to take them out to their ships and to a brand new world. Polly's orders read: "Report to your Commanding Officer." She followed orders and received this greeting: "Welcome aboard, Lieutenant. It is nice to have you. The corpsman will show you to your quarters."

After unpacking and waiting for the call for the noon meal, Polly heard male voices. "What am I hearing? Where are they? Can they see me?" Then she spied a small aperture. Unintentionally (for now) she listened to the gossip from above.

"How'd you do on this leave, Hank? Were the pickings good?"

"Were they! Man oh man! I laid a different broad each night. Next stop is Pearl, and I hear there are plenty of dames there. Trouble is, it takes a week to get there!" Hank then went on to name his conquests, elaborating as he did so.

Mischievously, Polly listened, hoping she could place a voice with Hank and in someway get even for his 'kiss and tell' antics. In the weeks ahead she did not bother to listen to the conversations from above, since all of them dealt with only one subject—sexual exploits. I must tell the other nurses about this, thought Polly, and don't let anyone ever tell me that men don't gossip as much as women!

The *Benevolence* had been at sea for a week now. That which had been new and exciting for doctor, nurse, corpsman and some of the crew was losing its enchantment. Since there were, as yet, no patients on board, most of the ship's inhabitants were on deck gazing westward for their first glimpse of land—and shore leave. Hank was very anxious to make his fantasy dreams a reality. Maybe, just maybe one of those hula girls he had heard about would place a lei around his neck, then lead him off to bed.

"Land!" cried someone. Officer and corpsman alike, although ready for leave, rushed to their quarters to put on the correct uniform and prepare for disembarkment.

Pearl Harbor, afloat with ships of all types and from all allied nations, was relatively quiet. Sunlit waves danced the hula hula over the graves of the *Arizona, Oklahoma, Utah, Tennessee* and the 2,403 men who lost their lives on that fateful day, December 7, 1941—a day which was to change the world forever. Over the harbor was an umbrella of fighter planes protecting the harbor from a possible kamikaze attack. None was expected at this distance from Japanese held territory, but the desperation of the Japanese following their naval defeat at Midway, gave birth to the kamikaze attack. They seemed bent on national suicide.

To the strains of "Sweet Leilani" Polly and her fellow officers disembarked and made their way toward officer quarters in Honolulu. As she walked through the door her face lit up with sudden joy! There was Jane waiting for Polly to arrive. Although only separated for a week, tears and laughter enjoined their embrace.

Their embrace was soon halted by the sight of a contingent of naval "brass" coming across the large vestibule. The young women knew what was coming, and what would be expected. The men were seeking a "companion" for the night.

"Quick, Jane, think of something! One of those officers coming toward us is undressing me garment by garment every step he takes."

"Let's hurry over there where Don is. He is a doctor whom I know, and will think of something," said Jane. They quickly hurried to Don, asking for his protection.

"Leave it to me if they come over here," said Don. "I will tell them that you are my girl, Polly, and that Jane is expecting her escort."

"Thank you, Don, you are a white knight in doctor's clothing. You know what could happen to us if we refused their advances. We were both just commissioned Lieutenant J.G."

"Are you sure you want to be rescued? They tell me that the one who had his eyes on you may be the next president of the United States." Don rolled his eyes then and said, "I can't say that I blame him for having his eyes on you!"

Polly smiled and took his arm. Both felt the strong stirring of physical attraction. Having a few days leave, they made a date to visit the graveyard of the ships sunk by the Japanese.

The next day Don and Polly strolled hand in hand close to the future site of the Arizona Memorial. In the waters below could be seen the still, gray forms of the sunken ships. Both stood in silence in deference to the men lying there.

"This was described as a 'Day of Infamy' by President Roosevelt. Didn't the navy have warning?" asked Polly very softly.

"Yes, they had plenty of warning. This should never have happened. It should be declared 'The Day of Neglect'. The officers in charge simply did not believe that this could happen. They, indeed, had their heads in the sand," replied Don. "If we had deliberately set ourselves up as targets, we could not have been more vulnerable." He pointed to where the ships had been anchored.

To the right of Ford Island were:

The *Solace* (A Hospital Ship)
2 Destroyers

31

The *Nevada*
The *Arizona*
The *Vestal*
The *West Virginia*
The *Tennessee*
The *Oklahoma*
The *Maryland*
The *Neosho*
The *California*

To the left of Ford Island were:
The *Detroit*
The *Raleigh*
The *Utah*
The *Tangler*

Over against the Army Reservation:
The *Argonne*
The *Audcet*
The *Oglala*
The *Helena*
The *Shaw*

Ships Sunk:
The *Arizona*
The *West Virginia*
The *Oklahoma*
The *Oglala*
The *California*

Those lost were:
2,086 Navy Personnel
237 Army Personnel
1,112 Civilians

3,435 Total

Don continued, "Polly, I know that you wanted to see this. I did, too, when I arrived. Let us now leave this scene of sadness and take a trip around the island, if they will allow us to do so."

Having been censored by the U.S. public for not listening to warnings of the Pearl Harbor disaster, the security measures were most stringent. Don and Polly had to settle for a trip to the Officer's Club.

CHAPTER VII

Jane, Flight Nurse

Jane's tour on a hospital ship ended when she arrived in Pearl Harbor. The next day she received, what were to her, thrilling orders. "Report to Hickham Field for indoctrination as a Flight Nurse." Whoopee! Now she would have a chance to learn to fly.

"I have always been a good driver," she said to Polly, "so I think I can fly all right, even though I will only fly in an emergency."

Polly was to learn later that Jane was not in the first squadron to go out, but soon followed, helping in the evacuation of the wounded from Okinawa. A description of a Flight Squadron follows:

Each twelve plane squadron operated with the following medical personnel[1]: one flight surgeon, twenty-four flight nurses, one hospital corps officer, and twenty-four pharmacists' mates. They worked tirelessly, flying out the wounded, sometimes having to circle the field for an hour or longer because the airstrips were under fire. Within thirty days, approximately 4,500 injured men were flown out of Okinawa.

An efficient procedure for aerial evacuation was developed. The squadron flight surgeon and several pharmacists' mates were in the first hospital plane to land on the field.

---

[1]*Army and Navy Nurses of World War II*, Military Publishing Co.

35

The surgeon established an evacuation clearing station adjacent to the airstrip where, with the help of corpsmen, he collected patients from first-aid stations and screened them for air transport, giving necessary treatment prior to flight. As soon as a hospital plane landed, the flight nurse received her orders. The plane was loaded and usually took off in about forty-five minutes after landing. With the aid of the corpsmen, she dressed wounds, administered whole blood or plasma, gave medications, fed and cared for the patients.

There were three main flights of air evacuation planes to which flight nurses were assigned overseas. First from target hospitals in Guam to Pearl Harbor, then from there to the continental United States. Nurses flight hours did not exceed 100 hours per month and were rotated from combat to non-combat zones.

All persons involved appreciated flight evacuation. Thousands of lives were saved due to the speed in which the wounded received the best of medical treatment. Appreciated by all was the use of antibiotics, but most appreciated by the wounded man was his NURSE.

When Polly and Jane met in Honolulu on the trip from San Francisco to Pearl Harbor, they formulated a plan whereby they might meet at Pearl during the war. They were to check in and out with the Chief Nurse of the Naval Hospital at Pearl. In that way they would know if they were there at the same time. They met only once, and that time the Chief Nurse saved them from the advances of officers on the prowl, since Don was not available.

CHAPTER VIII

Battle of Midway

The hot sun beat down on Edwards Air Force Base as Rick Masters pulled himself from the cockpit of the B17. It was noon and he would have a short respite from his duties as a flight instructor–his war-time job. Sometimes he felt frustrated and would have liked to be out there in the Pacific with the other fliers, some of whom he had taught to fly. He would like to show the Japs what a real flier could do. Then he shook his head. He knew that he really was doing a more important service for his country by teaching others to fly. He sighed and turned his thoughts to things more pleasant. He even laughed a little as he thought of how he had teased the men students by asking one of his women students to show them what a real take-off and landing should look like. Ida "Skip" Carter, a former Oklahoma State swimming champion, had unbelievable coordination and was very good indeed.

Now his thoughts turned, as they always did, to Polly. "Where are you, and what are you doing, my darling? Are you safe? Surely, even the Japs wouldn't sink a hospital ship–would they? Polly, I thought I would always be able to protect you. I love you enough for both of us! God, please take care of her."

By this time Rick had reached his office. On his desk was the morning paper. The headlines read: LT. COMMANDER JOHN C. WALDRON KILLED AT MIDWAY. Rick was shocked. Waldron, part Sioux, had been a friend of Rick's for many years. Soon after Pearl Harbor he became a folk hero to the American people. His forming of "The Torpedo Squadron Eight" into a very elite group of fighters had caught the imagination of Americans everywhere. In the first months of the Pacific War, America needed heroes, and John Waldron made good copy. The media particularly liked to repeat the story of how the Sioux Indian had taught his squadron to make scabbards for knives, and how to use those knives should they be forced down in the jungles of the islands.

The *Los Angeles Times* now emphasized that Waldron well knew that the Japanese fleet he was about to attack was at such a distance that the squadron could get there, destroy the enemy, but would not have enough fuel for the return trip. Two letters were found among his belongings—one to his squadron before their departure for the one-way trip, the other to his family. Below are those letters:

> "Just a word to let you know I feel we are ready. We have had a very short time to train and we have worked under the most severe difficulties, but we truly have done the best humanly possible. I actually believe that under these circumstances we are the best in the world. My greatest hope is that we encounter a favorable, tactical situation, but if we don't and the worst comes to the worst, I want each of us to do his utmost to destroy the enemies. If there is only one plane left to make a final run in, I want that man to go in and get a hit. May God be with us. Good luck, happy landings and give 'em hell."

His final letter to his family read:

> "Dearest Adelaide:
>
> "There is not a bit of news that I can tell you except that I am well. I have yours and the children's pictures here with me at all times.
> "I believe that we will be in battle very soon—I wish we were there today, but we are up to the eve of a very serious business. I wish to record to you

that I am feeling fine, my own morale is excellent and from my continued observance of the squadron–their morale is excellent also. You may rest assured that I will go with the expectation of coming back in good shape. If I do not come back–well, you and the little girls can know that this squadron struck for the highest objective in naval warfare–to sink the enemy.

"I love you and the children very dearly and I long to be with you, but I could not be happy ashore at this time. My place is here with the fight. I know you wish me luck and I think I will have it.

"You know, Adelaide, in this business of the torpedo attack, I acknowledge we must have a break. I believe that I have the experience and enough Sioux in me to recognize the break when it comes– and it will come.

"God bless you, dear. You are a wonderful wife and mother. Kiss and love the little girls for me and be of good cheer."

Love to all from Daddy
and Johnny"

Tears filled Rick's eyes as he said to himself, "When the time came, Johnny, you gave them hell, even though you knew it was a one-way trip. Happy landings, Johnny. I will look in on Adelaide and the girls."

CHAPTER IX

The Typhoons

How the sea swallows us,
our fears and treacheries,
without a word!

After each storm
we are lonely
as white birds
circling near the water.

Prior to World War II, very little was known about typhoons and the havoc they would wreak on the U.S. Navy and particularly the Third Fleet under "Bull" Halsey. Knowledge of the hurricane, which is born just north of the equator in the Atlantic Ocean, had been gained through many encounters. But not so the typhoon which is spawned where the tropical waters of the western Pacific join the waters of the China Sea. Most typhoons die in their early states, particularly if they meet cold water, but a few, where the conditions are right, grow, coiling like a mammoth snake striking with the force of an atom bomb. Such a typhoon hit the Third Fleet on January 17, 1944. There had been no warning since radar was not used for weather forecasting at that time. As a result, 780 lives were lost along with three destroyers and several ships.

41

In June of 1945 a two headed monster typhoon split in two, one hitting the *CV Hornet*, flagship of Rear Admiral Clark, with sixty foot waves causing the forward flight deck to collapse. While the *Hornet* was being repaired, Admiral Clark received word that two hospital ships were in distress and to send help. Admiral Clark decided to go himself. The *U.S.S. Benevolence* was one of the hospital ships.

Polly was scared. "I have never been so scared before, and hope never to be so scared again!" she said later.

The ship alert sounded. Then came the announcement, "This is your Captain speaking. We have been warned that we may be hit by very rough water and hurricane winds. All personnel report to your quarters for a life jacket. Nurses will then report to sick bay. A corpsman will come to escort you there."

Just then a giant wave hit the ship throwing Polly clear across her room. She managed to turn her body so that her buttocks hit the opposite wall, a maneuver she had learned in gym class at Classen High School in Oklahoma City. "Thank you, thank you, Miss Hulet," she said.

A corpsman appeared at her door holding onto anything available to keep his footing. Somehow he managed to let go with one arm so that he could salute. "May I escort you to sick bay, ma'am?" At that time, and under such adverse conditions, Polly recognized the voice, the voice which daily seemed to be piped into her quarters–the voice of Hank.

"Can we make it, do you think?" she asked.

"We have orders, we have to try," he said. "I am going to tie this rope around your waist and around mine. Now put your arm through mine. Here we go." Cautiously and slowly they made their way to sick bay where beds were anchored to the deck and patients anchored in their beds.

The *Benevolence*, not suited for such a storm, was in danger of capsizing. The captain struggled time and time again to keep the ship facing into the wind. Over and over the struggle was repeated. He managed to turn it sideways. At last, over the ship speaker came the announcement, "Admiral Clark is coming to our rescue. In the meantime, I suggest that all of us pray."

Doctors, nurses, and corpsmen knelt by the anchored beds praying and praying. Hank, who was kneeling by Polly, prayed. "Holy Mary, Mother of God, pray for this sinner."

The prayer went on and on and ended with, "If you save me, God, I promise to stop my womanizing."

"That is good," whispered Polly into his ear.

Hank looked at her in bewilderment. "How could she know?" he asked himself.

Hank did keep his promise to God during his next shore leave which occurred approximately two weeks after the typhoon. Then, being human, he proceeded to forget all about it.

On her next shore leave, Polly received a love letter from Rick:

Somewhere in the U.S.

"My love:

"YES, you are my one and only love, and I miss you with every breath I take. Until I met you, I never realized what love can do to a man.

"Last night on this desert I watched a beautiful sunset, and although you do not know it, you were there with me. We strolled into the sunset, as I hope we will do some day. Last night it was a land of magic. Dust in the air broke up the sun's rays, almost as raindrops from the rainbow. There were not the colors of the rainbow, but many were the shades of orange on the distant sky. I have never seen such vivid sunsets as we have here. I prayed, 'Please, God, let us meet the sunset of our lives together.' My dearest, as you are in my thoughts and dreams, I hope that I am in yours.

"Must now break this interval of day dreaming and return to the mundane. Am working from dawn to dusk with these young flyers. They are eager to learn and quickly master the mechanics of flying. Like all very young men, they lack patience. Although I keep saying, 'Have patience', I am afraid it is something which cannot be taught.

43

"Hope to get a few days leave soon. If so, will go where we last met and hope someone will have news of you.

All my love,

Rick"

CHAPTER X

The Bonzai Attacks

General MacArthur's strategy in the Pacific was to hop from one island to another, gobbling up each as he did so. His was a relentless march toward the Philippines where he had promised to return. His success made the Japanese desperate. Thousands of Japanese soldiers died in "Bonzai" attacks at Guadalcanal, Tarawa, Enietok and Attu. The worst kind of suicide charge was the "Gyokusai", or suicide charge in which the Japanese soldier was to take seven American lives before surrendering his own. Whether the Emperor actually called for "Gyokusai" on Saipan is not known, but the Japanese generals let the soldiers believe this to be true. The following document was found on the body of an officer after a "Gyokusai" attack. The message was from Lt. General Saito, Commander of the Japanese soldiers on Saipan:

"I am addressing the officers and men of the Imperial Army of Saipan. For more than twenty days since the American devils attacked, the officers, men and civilian employees of the Imperial Army and navy on this island have fought well and bravely. Everywhere they have demonstrated the honor and glory of the Imperial forces. I expected that every man would do his duty. Heaven has not given us the opportunity. We have fought in union up to the present time, but now we have no material with which to fight, and our artillery is com-

45

pletely destroyed. Our comrades have fallen one after another. Despite the bitterness of defeat, we pledge seven lives to repay our enemy.

"The barbarous attack of the enemy is being continued. Even though the enemy has occupied only a corner of Saipan, we are dying under the violent shelling and bombing. Whether we attack or stay where we are, there is only one death. However, in death there is life. We must take this opportunity to exalt true Japanese manhood. I will advance with those who remain to deliver still another blow to the American devils and leave my bones on Saipan as a bulwark of the Pacific."

However, Saito did not advance with his troops. He and Vice Admiral Nagumo, who was in command of the naval forces, committed the Japanese ritual of death, blood-letting, then were killed by aides with bullets to the head.

On July 7, 1944, the largest suicide charge of the war occurred. It is estimated that between 3,000 and 4,000 Japanese soldiers participated. Like stampeding cattle they came, trying to kill everything in their path. Supposed to be a three pronged attack, mostly it was one—down the coast.

One of the many surviving American casualties had been brought to the *U.S.S. Benevolence* for a severe abdominal wound. When sedatives allowed him to talk, he described his survival.

"We dug foxholes after we heard that the Japs were attacking that night or the next morning. At 5:10 a.m. we were hit by an avalanche of men. On and on they came. We were in our foxholes and they ran right over us. We fired into them until we ran out of ammunition. I tried to go to the next foxhole to get some, but all I saw there were Japs and Americans, some in hand to hand combat and some running south together. I crawled under some dead bodies. Then a single Jap came along and bayoneted me, even though I am sure he thought I was dead."

Polly shuddered. All morning reports had been coming in that hundreds of American soldiers, such as the one she was now treating, would soon be brought to the *Benevolence* and to other hospital ships in the region. She also heard that the dead, particularly the Japanese, were stacked like logs on the beach, where their bones would be left as a bulwark.

"That is a nasty wound you have there, soldier, but with the help of penicillin, you will soon be all right."

The soldier gave a sigh of relief and said, "It is so good to have a woman treating me. You are not old enough to be my mother, but it is as though she were here beside me."

Polly cleaned the wound, gave the soldier a shot of penicillin, then left the sick bay for composure. "Dear God," she asked, "why?" Then to herself she asked, could this war revealing man's inhumanity to man, have been averted? We are winning the war, she thought, but what will we have won? Thinking of the young men attacked on the beaches of Saipan, a wave of nausea hit her. As a surgical nurse, in Oklahoma City, she had aided in several amputations, but those had been the results of diseases or accidents, not intentional maiming by another man. Tears came to her eyes as she muttered, "I will never get used to this. The only reason I can bear it, is because I have to and that I am helping in the only way I know how."

CHAPTER XI

The U.S. Drops Atom Bombs on Japan

*Light of a thousand suns
and yet we are blind;
Shadows crossing a desert
of our own design.*

In 1939, around the world came rumors that the Germans had split the atom. Scientists everywhere were alarmed. If this were true, they soon could control the world.

Leo Szilard, a brilliant Hungarian physicist, was particularly alarmed. He and a fellow Hungarian went to see Einstein. Einstein listened and signed a letter to President Roosevelt asking that the United States begin research at once. When they could not seem to receive audience with the president, they went to Sachs, an advisor of the president. When Roosevelt did not see the problem as severe as others, Sachs told him, "Bonaparte might not have met his Waterloo, if he had listened to the young inventor of the steam engine, Robert Fulton. The French could easily have transported troops across the English Channel with the aid of the steam engine." Roosevelt laughed and gave the orders to immediately begin the work of splitting the atom.

In 1941, began the most extensive, scientific, industrial enterprise ever conducted by man. General Leslie R. Groves took command of an operation called The Manhattan Project, to transform equations, theory, and scientific knowledge (much of it provided by Einstein) into forming the atomic bomb. The leading physicist was J. Robert Oppenheimer. General Graves, who had been appointed by President Truman to head the project, drafted business magnates and coaxed incredible sums from Congress for the project.

Within months the American miracle was achieved. On the afternoon of December 2, 1942, under the football stands at the University of Chicago, the scientists produced the first chain reaction. They knew they had achieved the beginning of awesome destruction.

There were problems to be solved, however. The critical mass of U235, needed to develop the proper explosion, had to be determined. A laboratory for experimental purposes was necessary, one which would be away from any population center. Los Alamos, New Mexico was chosen with Oppenheimer as Scientific Director. No secret has been kept so well by so many as the development of the atomic bomb. The test site was fifty miles from Alamorgodo, New Mexico. The date was 5:50 a.m., July 16, 1945. The flash accompanying the explosion could be seen for 235 miles. To cover up the test, the following press notice was issued:

"An ammunition magazine exploded early today in a remote area of the Alamogordo Air Base Reservation, producing a brilliant flash and blast which was reported to have been observed as far away as Gallup, 235 miles northwest."

After the naval battle of Midway, where a large percentage of the Japanese navy had been destroyed, slowly and relentlessly the United States had moved forward, capturing and recapturing islands which would lead to the capture of the island of Japan. The loss of 750,000 lives was expected in the endeavor, especially now that the Japanese, in desperation, had resorted to kamikaze attacks by plane and by ships at sea. Many a Japanese took the one-way trip to death for love of country and emperor. An invasion was not to be, however.

During the "softening up" of Japan, Curtis E. Lemay's B29 bombers unloaded 40,000 tons of bombs, but only twelve of those had been dropped on the manufacturing city of Hiroshima. The death knell now sounded for this beautiful city.

"My God, what have we done?" said Robert A. Lewis, copilot of the *Enola Gay* which had just dropped the first atomic bomb. A genie, such as mankind had never known before was let out of its bottle by Captain Tibbets and the crew of the *Enola Gay*.

It is because of that genie that this book has been written. In the ensuing years since the dropping of the atom bombs the world has teetered on the balance beam of self destruction as the genie dances.

This writer will not go into the details of what happened on that day, August 6, 1945, except to say that 70,000 Japanese died, most of them cremated. The atomic bombing of Nagasaki soon followed. The Japanese had no choice but to surrender.

During the war years civilians knew not where their loved ones were, or what they were doing. All knew that the war was finally over—all that was left was the formal surrender of Japan. This civilian listened as she ironed clothes to ease the tension. Her heart jumped into her throat. Never would she forget the words:

"The formal surrender will be aboard the *U.S.S. Missouri* in honor of President Truman. Just off shore is the *U.S.S. Benevolence*. This hospital ship is taking aboard Americans and others who have been Japanese prisoners of war. One of these is General Jonathan Wainwright. We understand that the general said 'The sight of the beautiful navy nurses was the best medicine an American could have.' "

At the formal surrender was a long table holding the documents of surrender. To the right of the table stood the United States officers who had taken a leading part in the war. To the left of the table stood the stoic Japanese who never before had surrendered to any enemy.

Thus they stood for three to five minutes. Then on stage appeared the showman, General Douglas MacArthur. With him were Admiral Nimitz and Admiral "Bull" Halsey. By MacArthur's side, standing without support and as straight as possible, was the emaciated Jonathan Wainwright.

CHAPTER XII

War's End

The sound of the *U.S.S. Benevolence* cutting through the waves on its return from Tokyo to Pearl Harbor was music to those aboard, even those severely wounded or suffering from malnutrition. The song reverberated in ear and heart, "It is over! It is over!" No more mutilated bodies. No more young men crying "Mama," when engulfed with flaming oil. Tears of relief filled the eyes of nurse, corpsman and patient. Even the doctors were seen to shed a few tears.

Polly had managed to pull her mental curtain on something she knew would bring sorrow to both of them—she must tell Rick of her interest in and impending engagement to Don. "I cannot write a 'Dear John' letter to Rick. He deserves better than that," she said to herself.

In the meantime, Rick still on duty at Edward's Air Force Base, even though the war was officially over, held a letter from Polly in his hand. He had waited to read the letter until he could be alone in his office. The letter read, among other things, "I will call you when I get back to San Francisco. I must see you then."

Rick read between the lines. "I have lost her! Dear God, I have lost her! This damnable war separated us. I feel like flying out over the ocean and never coming back!"

Rick Masters, however, was a man who did not give up easily. "Until you are married, I will have hope, Polly, and you will be home soon. Maybe I can change your mind. I love you enough for both of us."

53

(The following chapters will be written in the first person—the author was there.)

Following the surrender of Japan, the United States celebrated—city, town, hamlet, and "wide open spaces in the road". Life seemed unreal. It appeared more difficult to adjust to peace than it had been to prepare for war.

It was with joy, however, that we received uncensored letters from our loved ones and discarded ration stamps for food and gasoline—particularly the latter. We were again a nation on wheels.

Polly wrote saying, "Will be in San Francisco in November for several days. Could you and Helen come down? I want you to meet Don."

My sister, Helen, and I decided to drive to San Francisco—a very foolish decision. Between Oregon and California is Mt. Ashland, often a problem in winter. Leaving after work, we reached the mountain at approximately 9:00 p.m. Snow and ice covered the road and thick fog hung above. Windows were rolled down and heads stuck out in order to see the yellow line. We drove down the center of the road on that yellow line all the way across the mountain. Yes, we were young and very foolish.

We arrived in San Francisco the next day just in time to hit the five o'clock traffic on the Bay Bridge, made our way to the St. Francis Hotel—and there was our Polly whom we had not seen for two years. Her face showed the strain of the war and dark circles were under the lovely eyes.

"Oh, Polly!" Helen and I exclaimed as both of us tried to gather her in our arms at the same time. "You look so tired—and sad."

At that, Polly broke into sobs, and with great difficulty said, "Rick just left. I had to tell him about Don."

"Are you sure, Polly?" I asked.

"I think so, and I had to make up my mind," she replied. "I hate to hurt someone as I have hurt Rick. He is such a wonderful man and so good to me. I do love him, but he does not make me feel the same as Don does. Don will be here before long to meet you two. I hope you like him."

When introduced to Don, I found him to be a very personable and interesting young man. Not so to my sister, Helen, who had always been somewhat psychic. She confided

54

in me, "Don't say anything to Polly, but I have a bad feeling about him."

Leaving Polly was difficult. To ease the pain, I had an idea. "Can you come to Oregon in June and go camping with us? I think our camping spot must be one of the most beautiful places in the world. It is at the confluence of Muir Creek with the Rogue River. If you can come, we can visit Crater Lake, go to Union Creek to Becky's for wild blackberry pie, see where the Rogue River disappears underground and just rest and sleep. You can wear some of my clothes for camping, but be sure to bring comfortable shoes."

When I returned to Oregon I wrote to her:

> "There is a place known to me that is like I think heaven will be. Time seems endless as the stream meanders through meadow and trees. Blue, blue are the many pools in which the wily trout lie. Perhaps if I cast just under the edge of yonder ledge? No, I cannot–there comes a fat beaver to see what I am doing here. Better move on to yonder rapids. As I move to the bank, where wild flowers abound, I receive a shock–the thunderous flight of a grouse escaping my feet. Soon soothed is my fast beating heart. Such is the power of this stream, named for John Muir–MUIR CREEK."

CHAPTER XIII

Camping

June arrived and so did Polly, but she had not taken my advice about clothes. She had new jeans, long sleeved shirts, sweaters, a rain coat for the Oregon weather, and camping boots. She would be the best dressed woman in camp! In a separate bag she had "dress up clothes". She would need them in Denver, where she planned on meeting Don when camping was over.

Polly, my friend, Betta, and I arrived at Muir Creek about noon the next day. All we had to do was set up one tent. Our camping companions were Clark and Glee Adams, friends for many years, and expert campers. I had previously told Clark, who was a former forest ranger, that I thought Polly, who had never camped before, would like to have a tent close to his protection. Her tent was all set up and ready. Polly was happy with her living quarters, and was delighted when Midge, the Adams' little Sheltie dog, decided it was her job to sleep in the small tent and protect the lovely new stranger.

The next day, as we did nearly every day, we went fishing. Polly looked at the bait—salmon eggs, worms and gravel bugs. I had an artificial fly on my pole. "I think I want one like yours," she said, looking at my pole.

Clark said, "I think you would have better luck with salmon eggs. They are not alive and they won't bite you. It takes a long time to learn to fly fish. I will put some eggs on your hook and show you how to do it." I left her in Clark's capable hands. Soon I saw that she was on her own and that she had gone down the Rogue, through a meadow where it is easy to fish. We heard a shout of glee and Polly came running. "Look, look what I caught," holding up an eight inch trout. "Come on down here. I've found a place where they are really biting!" And so she had, but most important of all, *THE CLOUDS OF WAR HAD BLOWN AWAY AND THE CHEERFUL SPIRIT OF POLLY SHONE THROUGH!* The vision of the clear, clear Rogue and the smell of the forest had brought peace to her heart.

That evening Betta went down to the Adams' camp to tell them dinner was ready–and that Polly's trout was among those cooked. She looked in the small tent. Midge was lying protectively close to her new love as Polly was again painting her fingernails a bright red!

"Do you think that will lure the fish?" asked Betta. "Dinner is ready. Are you?"

"Okay, I'll be there in a minute or so. I promised Midge that I would paint her toenails when I finished my own. Midge reached up to kiss her love and wagged her tail.

After dinner Clark added wood to the waning campfire. Our front sides would be warm for awhile. It would not be long before we crawled into bed to keep all our sides warm. As soon as the sun dropped below the horizon, the air at Muir Creek became cooler by the minute. By eight o'clock a jacket was needed, even if sitting by the fire. The fire flamed with the added wood and Clark squinted to avoid the rising smoke. "Were you in the Philippines when MacArthur returned in such dramatic fashion? He would have made quite a movie actor, don't you think?" Clark asked Polly.

"No, I was not there," Polly answered. "I heard from some of the men who were there that he was a little dramatic all right, but he really impressed the natives. The men under his command all agree that he is a great general. The one who impressed the nurses on the *Benevolence* was General Wainwright–the fact that he could stand during the whole surrender ceremony is astounding, considering how he was persecuted. He told us that he had not had a decent night's sleep in three and one-half years." She hesitated, thought for a while, then said, "If you folks would like to hear a story, I will tell you one."

"Yes, do," we all said.

"Okay," said Polly. "On my way to Pearl from Tokyo we docked at Naka, Okinawa. Our cousin, Frank Howard, a marine officer who had been in Pearl Harbor on that terrible morning of December 7, 1941, was now stationed in Okinawa and told this story about the first American court in Okinawa.

"On April 1, 1945 the United States Marines landed on the beach of Okinawa five miles north of Naha. The main body of the Japanese army was to the south. They had taken most of the civilians with them.

"Gradually the Japanese released the Okinawans and sent them north in U.S. trucks, eighty per truck, so stacked up that when a man died, he could not fall. Of the 377,000 Okinawans who had been there when the last census had been taken, only 283,000 remained. They evidently had been killed by American gunfire, as they were forced to serve in the Japanese army. Now the Americans were responsible for them and had to give them medical care, food and clothing.

"Military Government Units were established, and since there were very few senior officers present, many a twenty to twenty-five year old soldier governed 5,000 Okinawans. This included responsibility for housing, food, clothing, schooling, and constructing a water system.

"Generally, crime was not a problem, but one day it was reported that a husbandless young woman had given birth to a baby girl. Now, all of you know that in that part of the world, girls are not very important. The mother had no way to care for that baby so she smothered it with a pillow.

"No matter the reason, murder could not be permitted. Of the eighty American officers present, Frank and one other were the only ones with legal experience. The other officer acted as prosecutor. An Okinawan, who had attended in school in the U.S. and who had taken law classes at U.C.L.A., defended the woman. Frank acted as judge.

"Many spectators attended the trial, including twenty 'high brass' officers. When the court was called to order, all stood up. The defendant was asked to rise. According to Frank, she was scrubbed so clean her skin shone as much as her gleaming black hair which had been washed, then brushed over and over. She was dressed from the waist up in her very best—a shirtwaist made from her only dress. From the waist down, the marines had outfitted her in clean trousers, which needed

59

a rope at her waist to keep them from falling off, and shoes so large she could turn her feet completely around in them.

"The judge had to be sure, according to military law, that she understood the charges: WILLFUL MURDER.

"If found guilty, DEATH BY HANGING.

"When asked if she understood, the reply was "*ai*" (I understand.)

"The young woman spoke no English, Frank spoke no Japanese, yet, through an interpreter, a verdict was reached. GUILTY AS CHARGED.

"The sentence meted by the judge was three years imprisonment and a fine of one hundred dollars. (There was not one hundred dollars among all the natives.) The fine was suspended and the prisoner was assigned to laundry detail to be commuted after sixty days if her laundry work was satisfactory.

"The military government, including the 'brass' was very satisfied with the trial. Frank felt like Solomon."

By this time the fire was almost out and we all went to our tents, grateful the life of the young woman had been spared.

At 4,000 feet elevation, Muir Creek can get very cold in summer if certain conditions prevail. One year snow came to the higher mountains surrounding it on the Fourth of July! This year we were enjoying a week of sunshiny days and clear, very cold nights. Then rain came. Polly was cold. For many months she had been in tropical or semi-tropical climates and could not adjust to the sudden change in temperature. We decided to move to the coast where the weather would be warmer, even in case of rain.

So, we came down from the mountains to Grants Pass, where we could consult an authority on camping places, Betta's father, Robert Harris. I have never known a better camper or seen such a fisherman. He often stood in the center of the fast, cold McKenzie River, and cast close to the opposite bank. Remarkable! He very seldom left a creek or river without several nice trout.

Now he said, after much deliberation, "There is a forest camp just south of Humbug State Park–McGribble Forest Camp. Elk Creek, which is below, should be good fishing. Very few people are willing to walk down into that canyon, and it is worse to get out. Even if you do not fish, you can have a good time there. It is a short drive to Port Orford, one of the most beautiful spots on the coast, and you will be safe. The forest ranger's quarters are very close to camp. He will take good care of you, I am sure."

So we left our wet tent with Betta's dad, and borrowed a larger one from him. Polly would now sleep in our tent with us. She missed Midge and I am sure Midge missed her. We replenished our grocery supply at Grants Pass, then winding and unwinding the curvaceous road, we reached flat country where we drove through a large grove of redwoods before reaching Brookings and our first view of the ocean. The Oregon Coast, at Brookings, seems very peaceful. There is no surging and smashing of sea against rock as exists along most of Oregon's coastline, a coastline once described by Lowell Thomas as probably the most scenic in the world. Brookings had its own beauty on this day, the speciosium lilies in bloom. They looked like acres and acres of orchids. Polly said, "This must be Shangrila!"

We arrived at McGribble Forest Camp about 4:00 p.m., just soon enough to set up camp. The forest ranger, noticing no men were around, came down from his cabin, about 200 yards up the mountain, to offer his assistance. He helped set up the tent and brought wood. To say thanks, we invited him to a dinner of steak, fried potatoes and a green salad, since on this, our first evening away from Grants Pass, we had a full larder. The ranger said, "I really appreciate this meal and the good company."

"We are happy to have you," Polly replied.

"Is Elk Creek good fishing?" Betta asked.

"Sometimes," he said, "but the trail leading there is about one-half mile straight down, and very difficult to climb down and worse to climb back up. I'm not sure you should go there. My advice is to not try it unless you are in excellent physical shape."

We talked it over. Betta and I could make it, as we had gone into more difficult situations on the McKenzie River, but Polly? She spoke up, "I want to try it."

The next morning, early, we walked up to the beginning of the trail. And there, for all of us to see, was the sign, "KILROY WAS HERE!" We went down that very steep trail and decided any fish in the creek could just stay there. We wanted to be sure we had time to climb out. With difficulty

61

we climbed back to the place Kilroy had been, then slowly dragged our weary selves back to camp.

Somewhat tired, and very stiff the next day, we decided to enjoy city life and the beach. We knew Polly would enjoy seeing the scenic, small town of Port Orford and to stroll the beach. We would not swim—very few people swim in the Oregon ocean, because of the water temperature. We strolled the beach that day, the only occupants, watching the breakers hit and curl over and around the huge rocks. The raucous cry of the seagull added a new decibel of sound to the scene. Civilization with its foibles, pleasures, and heartbreak belonged to another time and place. So beautiful it was, we loitered and extended each minute as long as possible.

On our way to and from camp, we had noticed an abandoned apple orchard—apparently planted by early settlers, and now so loaded with apples, the branches touched the ground. We picked as many as we could carry, scolding ourselves that we had not brought pails to carry more.

That night, over the campfire, we cooked fried apples, fried potatoes, and bacon. We were all so very hungry, having had only a sandwich at noon, that we cooked lots of bacon and potatoes, and all the apples we had picked. Just as we finished cooking, a sudden rain moved in. It was not a hard rain, but a penetrating mist. It was enough that we had to take our plates and move to the tent. Betta grabbed the old iron skillet containing a small amount of fried apples left over after filling our plates. We finished eating and looked longingly at the few apples left in the skillet. We must all be commended for our unselfishness. When we were asked if we would like the remaining apples, each of us said no. I apportioned the apples to each plate. Then we all three laughed.

The rain had moved inland by the next morning, and the sun was shining. We were happy about that, as there is nothing worse than trying to pack up from a camping trip in the rain.

We took our time before packing, and while enjoying breakfast, an incident happened which I will never forget. About twenty feet away, sat the largest rat I have ever seen. While sitting it appeared, as I remember, about eighteen inches high. It was frightening. Forty years later I have learned that it was probably a mountain beaver!

62

We wished we could drive on up the entire coast, so that Polly could enjoy the sights, smells and friendly people we would encounter, but we had to return to Eugene. From there she would fly to Denver to meet Don.

Before leaving, she said, "I have received orders to go to the Bikini Atoll for the atom bomb tests."

Startled, I said, "Oh no, Polly!"

She said, "It is all right. All safety precautions will be taken. I will be all right."

CHAPTER XIV

Prison Camps

Very little word had reached the outside world from the prison and internments in Japanese control. Now that the war was over, the news of conditions and atrocities were being spread over the "civilized" world. Polly, arriving in San Francisco, following her trip to Denver, had purchased a copy of *Army and Navy Nurses of World War II.*[1]

In her quarters, aboard the U.S.S. *Benevolence,* she sat on her bed crosslegged, reading about the nurses who were prisoners in one of the camps. "Oh, Dear God," she exclaimed as she looked at pictures of the nurses on their arrival in San Francisco following the surrender of Japan. They were so very thin that the dresses they had made by hand, from worn out dungarees, hung loosely. The curves of womanhood were missing. From time to time her eyes went back to the picture as she read: "Months prior to Pearl Harbor, some civilians and dependents of service men had been evacuated, but many stayed on."

On December 8, 1941, twelve navy nurses and three civilian nurses were stationed at the Naval Hospital, Canacao, near Manila Bay. Chief Nurse, Laura M. Cobb, was in charge. She and ten others had stayed on to help the hundreds of army and navy wounded. One navy nurse, who had been with an army surgical team at Corregidor, escaped

---

[1]*Army and Navy Nurses of World War II,* Military Nurse

to Australia by submarine. When she returned to the United States in 1942, she was the first member of the naval service to receive the Legion of Merit.

By New Year's Day 1942, Japanese troops captured the entire naval medical unit, and during the next eight weeks many men were sent to military prison. The women were sent to Santo Tomas, a civilian internment camp. The camp was heterogeneous, having all ages, including 300 children. Dr. C.M. Leach of the Rockefeller Foundation, a member of the camp, was put in charge of the camp hospital. Due to poor nutrition and lack of sanitation, many prisoners became ill.

Then in May 1943, at Los Banos, sixty miles from Manila, the Japanese set up a new prison camp. Dr. Leach again became the medical director. The navy and civilian nurses went with him. The medical supplies were so limited that Yankee ingenuity was tested, coming up with the following: beds, tables and other furniture were made with bamboo and wood; medical and cooking utensils came from corrugated tin; drinking glasses came from old bottles where the necks had been carefully broken off; the bottle necks served as "call bells", with a piece of metal for a "clapper", fastened by a strong vine; an instrument sterilizer was improvised from an old piece of tin and bandages were sterilized by washing and ironing; precious medicines were dispensed frugally; sap from nearby trees was used for adhesive plaster.

During internment, 150 major surgical operations were performed including two Caesarian operations. By 1945, food had become so scarce, many starved. One or two deaths a day were common. Near the end, burial waited until someone strong enough to dig a grave was found. No dog, cat, or rat was safe during the last months.

Most of the above information came from a diary recorded by Chief Nurse Laura M. Cobb who also gave this account of their release from prison:

"Finally, release came! Early in the morning, according to one of the nurses, came the rumbling of planes and I saw a parachute open. I thought it was food, but soon saw one parachute following another dropping. The cry went up 'Parachutists!'

"Firing began on the outer rim of the camp, and realizing there would be casualties, I went downstairs to sterilize instruments. The camp was caught in a crossfire and we looked for shelter. I found a spot at the kitchen window and watched the action. Tanks began approaching and someone yelled, 'Jap tanks!'

"But jeeps started rolling out of those tanks and we knew they were ours. Those American men looked so big, so fat and so good!

"After caring for the wounded in camp, the nurses made their escape, under fire, in jeeps and tractors."

Polly, tears streaming down her face, quietly said, "Maria, Maria, thank God!"

CHAPTER XV

The Bikini Atoll

Loosely fixed in warm blue waters
where only sun and rain
for thousand years
had blessed them,
a shining coral world is lost,
a home destroyed
in scattered flashes
of sickening light,
a culture displaced, again,
in the brutal sweep of blindness.

Hank and Polly, who together had faced and escaped death from the typhoon Cobra, were now good friends. From Polly, Hank had acquired an appreciation for womanhood, unknown to him previously. He came to her now for information.

"Commander, ma'am, may I talk with you?" asked a very serious Hank Miller.

"Since you escorted me to safety during that typhoon we both endured, yes, you can talk all you wish, Ensign," replied Polly.

"Bikini Atoll—what is an atoll, ma'am?"

Polly replied, "When I heard we were going there I read several books, and here is some of the information I gathered: an atoll is an upper part of a long pillar of limestone extending thousands of feet down into the ocean where it is securely fastened to the crater of an extinct volcano. The volcano was once at sea level, but as it sank, coral which formed around it, built new cells on top in order to survive. As the old coral sank it became solid limestone. These pillars are probably a million years old. At the surface of the atoll itself, is a living coral organism in the shape of a ring formed around a lagoon of unbelievable beauty. The water is an emerald green. Come back tomorrow, Hank, and I will tell you more of the things I learned."

That night in her quarters Polly read on and on about the Pacific Atoll. It was fascinating reading.

The next morning when Hank arrived for his lesson, Polly told him what she had read:

"Debris accumulating on the windward side of the atoll, gradually produced soil. In the soil, babai was planted and cultivated–babai being the 'sacred' food of the atoll people. It was not sacred as expressed in current terminology, but sacred because it was important for sustenance of life. The atoll people lived on babai, fish and whatever fruit grew on the atoll.

"Land was and is the most important possession to a man on an atoll, but no man is allowed to own more than his neighbor. If a man acquires more than the atoll society thinks is proper, he is ostracized.

"The atoll people had another very interesting habit called *bamboose*, meaning: to give, borrow, lend, share, part with. The word *must* is understood to preface the preceding verbs. If asked to do any of the above, the individual must comply. Bamboozing can only be done by a relative, but this meant nearly everyone, as most inhabitants on the atoll are related."

Hank then asked, "Commander, ma'am, did you read anything about the women? Are they beautiful?"

Polly answered, "Hank, I do not know, but remember your promise to God when we were in that typhoon. Be careful. Remember these are innocent women, like children. Treat them gently, as you would children. I also must tell you that those who are beautiful, will not remain that way long. Soon they will have sagging breasts and shuffle when they walk.

Hank hesitated, then said, "I will do as you say, ma'am, and thank you for telling me this. I am scared. Some of the fellows say we will be killed or sterilized. Will we?"

"No, I do not believe so. I am sure that every precaution will be taken to prevent such a thing," replied Polly, trying to calm Hank's fears. Inwardly, she was not so sure.

She remembered Nagasaki. She and other naval personnel had been allowed to get close enough to that once lovely city to see the devastation wreaked by the atom bomb. Such sights are not soon forgotten, and it was with apprehension that she heard the navy was to conduct experimental tests at sea. Two bombs were to be dropped, one from overhead as at Nagasaki, the other to be detonated under water.

This experimentation would take place at the Bikini Atoll a group of small islands in the Pacific Ocean. The fleet was to give assistance, if needed.

She and other nurses who were there at the Bikini experiment, talked very little about it. It was as though it was something they wished to forget. Polly said, "Our ship was approximately fifteen miles away. We were told that we could come on deck if we would close our eyes, then put an arm over them. I did and every bone in my arm was x-rayed." (That was on Abel Day.)

Most of the knowledge of what happened at Bikini comes from a film documentary, "Radio Bikini", Robert Stone Productions, Ltd. and from the book, *No Place to Hide* by Dr. David J. Bradley. Dr. Bradley was a radiological monitor at Bikini.

Authentic navy pictures and authentic sound gathered by Mr. Stone over a period of four years are used in the film.

From the documentary: "We hear the naval officer in charge ask, through an interpreter, permission from the King of Bikini, Kilion Bauno, to drop the bombs after all natives have been evacuated. Several times we hear the naval officer say, "Tell him it is for the good of mankind."

Forty plus years later when interviewed for the documentary, King Bauno said, "They told us it was only temporary. They lied. Our homeland is everything to us. I want to go back there, but I can't go. They say it is poisoned."

So, FOR THE GOOD OF MANKIND, little goats were tied in stanchions to see how or if they would survive the explosions. Did the navy not know from Nagasaki? From a distance servicemen were allowed to lie on deck, face up, with only protective goggles over their eyes when the bomb was dropped. Following the explosion, we heard the rat-tat-tat of the geiger counter reacting to the radioactive belts of those servicemen.

Next, the navy conducted an underwater bomb explosion. This *was* the first time such a thing had been done and proved to be a terrible disaster. Radioactive water shot into the air, inundating ships and personnel. This writer believes that the navy ran scared. They pulled out as quickly as possible, but not before thousands of servicemen and women had been covered with radioactive material.

From the documentary we hear an interview with John Smitherman, a sailor who was aboard one of the ships. Over a period of forty years he suffered from an undiagnosed disease, causing arms and legs to swell so much the skin ruptured. The doctors, knowing not the cause or the treatment, amputated both legs. Mr. Smitherman said, "We did not know anything about the radiation. We thought it was a wonderful thing we were doing, and we were proud to be a part of it. We were in awe when we saw that column of smoke rise over 10,000 feet into the air. We had no idea of the danger involved when we were allowed to swim and go wash our clothes in the radioactive water." (Mr. Smitherman may not have used these exact words.)

Dr. David Bradley in his firsthand account of the atomic tests at Bikini–*No Place to Hide*–gives, as far as the author knows, the most detailed description that has ever been given of such a test. His description of Baker Day, the underwater detonation, and the consequential death blows dealt the ships anchored there, brings fear to any reader. He describes the aircraft carrier *Independence* arriving in San Francisco not long ago. She is now an outcast ship, the disease of radio activity on her decks, sides and corridors. As Dr. Bradley says, "She was anchored off shore in strict isolation, a leper."

CHAPTER XVI

Discovery of Cancer

On October 12, 1947, a little over a year following the Bikini bomb experiment, Helen called me from Hollywood, where she was then living. Polly had been admitted to Corona Naval Hospital complaining of a lump in the left breast. She had noticed it about seven weeks previously. On biopsy the lump was found to be malignant. A radical mastectomy was performed October 20, 1947 at the Long Beach Naval Hospital. The operation revealed that the lymph nodes were extensively involved with metastasis. On November 13, a lump was discovered in the right breast. The breast was removed, although the lump was benign. When treated by deep x-ray, she suffered severe gastro-intestinal reactions, loss of appetite and secondary anemia.

I went down at Christmas time and made arrangements to bring her home with me in the spring. She, of course, had retired from the navy.

When spring finally arrived and school was out, I drove to California. She was feeling much better and had had a good summer. Following the operation, she had been informed by the medical staff that the operation had been so extensive, she would probably be unable to use her left arm. This brave young woman fooled the experts. Three or four times a day she combed her hair with her left hand, developing muscles until her use of the left arm appeared almost normal.

The duplex apartment Helen, Polly, and I rented that summer in Culver City was in no way elegant, but was comfortable and well protected. The police station was next door! It was also close to a grocery store and to Hal Roach Studios where Helen worked, not as a movie star but as a secretary. However, she knew many of the movie stars, of course–Ingrid Bergman, being one. Another was one from another era, Bebe Daniels. Miss Daniels took a fancy to Helen, often had lunch with her, and when the movie was finished, gave Helen a beautiful necklace with matching earrings.

One summer morning we heard a desperate ring of the doorbell. In pajamas and robes we answered. The young woman next door stood there, anxiety etched on her face. She turned to Polly. "I know you are a nurse. Can you help me? My cat is giving birth to kittens and seems to be in serious trouble. These are her first kittens."

We all went next door and "Cully" (named after Culver City) indeed was in trouble.

"Can we take her to the vet in your car?" she asked me.

"Of course," I said.

We quickly put on slacks, Polly crawled into the back seat with Cully, who was on towels borrowed from the two apartments, and off we went. The vet delivered the kittens, one black, and one black and white, one gray and one calico. No fathers could be found. The young woman who owned Cully was very worried about the vet bill. How would she pay it? Helen, Polly and I offered to pay.

Polly said, "I am the one who brought her here, so I should be the one to pay the bill of $100.00."

I said, "We were all in on this, so all of us will pay."

All during this conversation I noticed that Polly had her eyes on a little black kitten in a nearby cage. She had white feet and a white diamond on her chest. She looked as though she might be part Siamese from the shape of her ears and the look in her eyes. Polly picked her up and the little animal immediately started sucking on Polly's arm. Polly was a "goner". Of course we took that little black kitten home with us with the vet's blessing. We named her Ginger. She was to play a big part in all our lives in the coming year.

Medical society is just now finding how much a little animal can play in the mental health of those who are in need of companionship, or how one can take an ill person's attention away from his illness. Ginger was an artist at this.

She would allow no "sleeping in". When the time arrived that she thought we should feed her, or at the very least pay her some attention, she first jumped on the coffee table near the divan on which one of us slept, and began twirling the silver ash trays or other movable objects around. If we still slept, she knew just what to do. She began rattling the venetian blinds, then if we still stayed in bed, she started climbing up the blinds! Then, of course, we jumped out of bed and fed her. We taught her to retrieve. The rolled up cellophane wrapper from a cigarette package made a good ball for a kitten. I hesitate to say how many times such a ball was thrown, retrieved by Ginger, then brought back and placed in or on our shoes to be thrown again.

About four weeks after we adopted Ginger, the vet called saying that Cully was ready to bring home. All her kittens had been adopted. She and Ginger immediately became friends. Cully's owner worked, so we often brought her in to play with Ginger. They chased one another all over the apartment. Then one day, when Cully's owner was home, we decided to take the two cats out in our rather large back yard. Cully was evidently glad to have mother earth for her bathroom needs. She proceeded to dig a hole in the ground, relieve herself, then to cover it up. All of us have seen a cat perform this ritual many times, but Ginger had never seen such a thing. She was bug-eyed. She watched carefully, then proceeded to go all around that back yard digging holes, sitting on them leaving no residue, but carefully covering up each one. You can be sure she had our undivided attention!

To come back with me to Oregon at summer's end, Polly insisted that she needed a steamer trunk, such as stage people use when travelling. It would hold all the pretty clothes she had managed to buy some way, somehow. To find the needed trunk, she and I read the classified section of the Los Angeles Times the first thing each morning, then drove to examine the steamer trunks which were advertised. It took about two weeks to find the one she wanted, in a city filled with stage and motion picture people and steamer trunks! It was very handy, however, and when we arrived in Eugene, we used the trunk as an extra closet.

Polly was, by this time, feeling well enough to enroll at the University of Oregon. However, enrollment was all she managed, for soon afterwards she began having severe back pain. She knew she needed help. Bremerton, Washington, being the closest Naval Hospital, she checked in there. The doctors there suggested that she return to Long Beach. This she did, taking that steamer trunk with her. She planned on staying with Helen when and if she left the hospital.

CHAPTER XVII

The Vigil

Polly had started school at the age of four, primarily because our mother was her teacher and could be with her. When unable to be with her, the job fell to me. I, only four years older, was a second mother to my little sister. When our mother died at age fifty from a ruptured appendix, Polly turned to me for comfort. Now that her life had been devastated, she again turned to me. My sister Helen called from Hollywood saying, "Polly is calling for you." I went, of course. How lucky I was to have an understanding principal and that the Eugene, Oregon School Board was very humane. I was also lucky to have a reliable substitute.

In 1949, in the gray fortress hospital in Long Beach, California, Polly awaited death from terminal cancer. How very difficult it is to write this—even after forty years. This being so, I will not dwell on her pain and suffering. However, I believe one very strange phenomenon should be mentioned —a vibration, similar to ripples of electricity occasionally emanated from her body. I have no idea why this happened. As far as I know, the Chief Nurse and I were the only ones to feel this. I mentioned it to her one day, and she said, "Oh, so you have felt that, too. I don't know why that should happen."

In spite of Polly's suffering, somehow this brave young woman managed at times to become the joyous young woman described in Chapter I. One day when I heard laughter as I approached her room, I stuck my head in and asked, "What is going on in here?" Joe E. Brown, the famous comedian, was there visiting with her.

Polly said, "I was telling Mr. Brown all about you. I informed him that Helen and I had an agreement that in our old age she and I would be the lively old ladies at the end of the hall in some retirement home, and that you would support us."

Joe E. Brown, bless his heart, came every day after that, stayed about thirty minutes, then left with his well-known open mouth farewell.

The navy Hospital at Long Beach was still at war–a battle against cockroaches. Insects of all kinds like the California climate. Cockroaches, particularly, thrive in kitchens or any place food is stored. Many went scurrying to safety when I went out early in the morning for a cup of coffee.

I told Polly about this and she said, "I will have to get out of this bed, call them to attention, then lead them down the hall and out of the building."

During the first few weeks after my arrival, Polly waited for Don to come. He never did. Could it be that he thought she would still wish to marry him? I think not. We all know that some men cannot seem to face pain in themselves or others, but most call upon reserve strength when a person they love is involved. Don could not, or did not do so. In these forty years since Polly's illness, I have found it very difficult to forgive him. Philosophically, however, I have convinced myself that if there is a reason for Polly's premature death, it may be that she was spared from marrying Don and probably having many unhappy years.

Jane somehow managed to get a month's leave and came to be with her best friend. Polly let her relieve me of some nursing duties. Nurses were on duty around the clock on each floor, but Polly wanted only Jane or me.

One day Jane fastened an orchid to the foot of Polly's bed. Polly seemed very pleased. For some reason, known only by the two of them, she remarked, "You didn't forget."

One day, Polly asked, "Do you suppose Rick could come?" I called him. That blessed man said, "I will be there."

Happiness lit up Polly's face and pervaded the hospital room when Rick arrived. Gently he gathered the frail body in his arms, saying over and over, "My darling little girl, how I love you."

"Even the way I look now?" asked Polly whose hair was now salt and pepper and her parchment skin yellow, as is the case with liver cancer.

"You will always be beautiful to me, so very beautiful, especially the beauty radiating from within," replied Rick.

Polly gave a sigh of contentment, then said, "No woman has been loved more, or by so wonderful a man. How different you are from Don."

Rick replied, "We must not think of unpleasant people or unpleasant things now."

Jane said, "You can say that again."

Rick took up the death vigil with Helen, Jane and me. When Polly's heart, which had been strong, finally stopped September 3, 1949, the orchid at the foot of her bed tumbled sideways.

REQUIEM FOR POLLY GLINES

Is it the eyes we remember, dear Lord,
the lost and empty eyes of Nagasaki?

Is it the downcast gaze of the Bikini islanders
who forty years later, cannot go home?

Is it the distant stare of our own countrymen,
following orders,
that would so alter the course of history?

You, of the warm and loving eyes, Polly,
witness to all this darkness,
how could your life contain these sorrows,
these terrible insults of time and place?

When that fragile air could no more
breathe within you,
when the sickness had claimed your body,
leaving those present with their thoughts,
thoughts, which even now flood us
like a swollen Oregon stream,
you close your eyes
to this once so lovely world.

Was there some good reason for your dying
dear Polly, or for all those others?
Were you victims of some awful mistake?
Even now, adrift in the present,
where we survive,
burying our losses over and over,
there are generals, and worse,
who would do it all again, on a dare,
men whom we know,
have never seen the glow of love
in our sister's eyes,
in our brother's tearful eyes.

Tom DeLigio

EPILOGUE

GOD FORGIVE THEM FOR THEY KNEW NOT WHAT THEY WERE DOING!

It cannot be *proved* that the underwater explosion of an Atomic Bomb at the Bikini Atoll, on Baker Day, Thursday, July 25, 1946 caused Polly's death. Nor can it be *disproved.*

No one knew then, nor does anyone know now, all the consequences of such an experiment. How many of the 40,000 service men and women, who were there on that day, have died premature deaths? This author knows of four. Medical science would agree, I am sure, that a geyser of radioactive water which shot several thousand feet into the air, then fell back to the sea, inundating both ships and personnel, would probably cause some cancer. At Bikini, this was followed by a "rain" of the radioactive material, lasting for about twenty minutes.

What are we doing? What have we done? If we do not harness this force, so that tests as well as its use are safe, we can only destroy this planet and its inhabitants. The "atom genie" can dance either a life ritual or a ritual of death.